P9-CNH-269

Simon & Schuster Books for Young Readers
New York London Toronto Sydney

To Brian Buerkle—M. C.

Thanks to Stacy Buerkle, former first-grade teacher extraordinaire,
who provided valuable input on the manuscript—M. C.

SIMON & SCHUSTER BOOKS FOR YOUNG READERS
An imprint of Simon & Schuster Children's Publishing Division
1230 Avenue of the Americas, New York, New York 10020

Book design by Daniel Roode
The text for this book is set in AGaramond.
The illustrations for this book are rendered in watercolor on paper.
Manufactured in China
2 4 6 8 10 9 7 5 3 1
Library of Congress Cataloging-in-Publication Data
Cuyler, Margery.
Hooray for Reading Day! / Margery Cuyler ; illustrated by Arthur Howard.—1st ed.
p. cm.
Summary: First-grader Jessica, a big worrier, is especially afraid that she will make a mistake when she is reading in front of her class and parents on Reading Theater day, but after lots of practice reading to her dog Wiggles, she performs perfectly.
ISBN-13: 978-0-689-86188-8 (hardcover)
ISBN-10: 0-689-86188-5 (hardcover)
[1. Worry—Fiction. 2. Reading—Fiction. 3. Schools—Fiction. 4. Dogs—Fiction.]
I. Howard, Arthur, ill. II. Title.
PZ7.C997Re 2008
[E]—dc22
2007005191

Jessica was a worrier.
She worried all the time.

She worried about monsters under her bed

and getting a haircut

and going to the dentist

and remembering to walk Wiggles.

But in first grade, she had a BIG worry. Reading!

Mr. Martin had divided the class into small groups.

When it was Jessica's turn to read, she had trouble sounding out the words. She read c-c-c-cat for cat and d-d-d-dish for dish.

Sometimes the other kids laughed, and Jessica turned as red as a radish.

"Stop making fun," Mr. Martin said to the group. Then he asked Jessica to go back to the beginning and try again.

Jessica hated it when he said that. What if she made another mistake?

One morning, Mr. Martin gave the kids a book called *Hot Pot*.

"Please read the first sentence out loud," he said to Jessica.

Jessica’s stomach flip-flopped.
“Can I go last?” she asked.
“If that will help,” said Mr. Martin.

“Dot had a pot,” read Anita.

“The pot had a sp-spot,” read Leslie.

“Dot put the pot on a cot,” read Bobby.
What a dumb story, thought Jessica.

“Your turn,” said Mr. Martin.
Jessica took a deep breath.
“The p-p-pot was *snot,*” she read.
Everyone laughed at her mistake.
Jessica wanted to sink into the floor.

"Shhh," Mr. Martin said to the class.

Then he turned to Jessica. "Try again. I know you can do it."

Jessica looked down. The words swam around the page. She closed her eyes so that the words would stop swimming.

Then she opened her eyes and read, "The p-p-pot was h-h-hot."

"Much better!" said Mr. Martin.

The next morning Mr. Martin announced, “Friday is Reading Theater day. I want each of you to read a line from your books out loud. And I want you to dress up in costumes. That will make it more fun. I’ve invited your parents, and we’ll have cupcakes and juice.”

Jessica's stomach turned a somersault.

Read out loud? Wear a costume? She thought she'd rather get a splinter in her tongue than do that!

At dinner that night, Jessica didn't feel like eating.
"What's wrong?" asked Mom.
"Everything," said Jessica.

“Go on,” said Dad. “Tell us.”

Jessica sighed. “Mr. Martin said he invited the parents to Reading Theater.”

“That’s right,” said Mom. “We’re looking forward to it.”

“Not me,” said Jessica. “I don’t want to read in front of a bunch of strangers. Especially a line from a *dumb* story about a cot and a pot. And I definitely *don’t* want to wear a costume.”

“Why not?” said Mom. “I had to do that once. It wasn’t easy, since I was the slowest reader in first grade. Then one day everything clicked, and I became the best reader in the class!”

“Oh,” said Jessica.

"I'll help you with your costume," said Laura. "You can dress up as a sheet."

"Or a pillow," added Tom.

"*Very* funny," said Jessica.

That night Jessica couldn't sleep.
Words floated around in her head.
Hot. Pot. Snot.
Spot. Dot. Cot.

Finally she turned on the light. Wiggles woke up and licked her face.

"Stop that," said Jessica. Then she got an idea. "Hey, maybe I'll practice on you."

She opened her backpack and pulled out her copy of *Hot Pot*. Wiggles snuggled up next to her.

Jessica opened the book and began to read. "Dot had a pot. The pot had a spot. Dot put the pot on the cot. The pot was hot."

Jessica looked at Wiggles.

"I didn't make any mistakes!" she said. "It's easy to read to you."

The next day Mr. Martin asked Jessica to read out loud. Jessica mixed up some of the words.

"Pot had a dot," she read.

Everyone giggled.

“Don’t worry,” said Mr. Martin. “It’s not the end of the world if you make a mistake.”

But to Jessica, it was. She’d have to practice all day and all night for Reading Theater.

When Jessica got home, she read to Wiggles. She read the whole story through without making any mistakes. Wiggles gave her doggy kisses.

"Maybe if I can read to you," said Jessica, "I can read to anybody. If Mom learned to be a good reader, why can't I?"

"Arf! Arf!" barked Wiggles.

Finally it was the day of Reading Theater. Jessica went to school wrapped in a blanket. When the parents began to arrive, Jessica put the blanket over her head.

Mr. Martin greeted everyone. Then he asked Jessica's group to stand up. Jessica kept the blanket over her head as she walked to the front of the classroom.

Anita read first,

then Leslie.

Next it was Bobby's turn.

"Tod put the top on a splot," he read.

Jessica threw off her blanket. She stared at Bobby. He had made a mistake. He never made mistakes! And now it was her turn!

Jessica's knees shook. She closed her eyes and pictured Wiggles. Then she opened her eyes and pretended she was reading to him. "THE POT WAS HOT!" she read.

Phew! She had got it right! She closed the book with a bang and sat down.

The parents all clapped.
So did the other kids.
Mom and Dad clapped loudest of all.

"You were great!" said Mom.
"Hooray for Reading Day!" said Dad.
"Bravo," said Mr. Martin. "I knew you could do it!"
Jessica smiled.

That night she read another story to Wiggles. And then another. And another.

Wiggles licked the book.

"You must like this story!" said Jessica.

Then she gave him a big hug and they both fell asleep.